William Amphlett

The Triumphs of War

William Amphlett

The Triumphs of War

ISBN/EAN: 9783744716130

Printed in Europe, USA, Canada, Australia, Japan

Cover: Foto ©Andreas Hilbeck / pixelio.de

More available books at **www.hansebooks.com**

THE

TRIUMPHS OF WAR:

AND

OTHER POEMS.

BY

W. AMPHLETT.

——————————————— even *now,*
When Science roams at large about the world,
When men would fain be thought exceeding wise,
And talk of reason and religion too,
As though their hearts felt what their tongues repeat,
Even *now*, the monster triumphs!
Triumphs of War, *p.* 53.

LONDON:
PRINTED BY C. WHITTINGHAM;
SOLD BY S. BAOSTER, NO. 81, STRAND; AND J. PARSONS,
PATERNOSTER ROW.
1796.

ADVERTISEMENT.

————

THE following poetical Essays are the first production of a young person, born and educated in the country, and who has resided for some time past in the vicinity of the metropolis; but has never enjoyed the advantages of academical instruction. They are the fruit of much miscellaneous reading, and some observation, the offspring of a warm imagination, and a susceptible heart. Should this Volume in any degree attract the public attention, and he be thereby induced to make a farther exertion of his powers at any future period; he will sedulously avail himself of that assistance, which the remarks of the learned, the judicious, and the candid, cannot fail to afford him.

LONDON,
May 20, 1796.

CONTENTS.

THE TRIUMPHS OF WAR.

A POEM.

———

NOT of Idalian groves, or bowers of bliss,
Or limpid streams Arcadian prospects yield ;
Not of all-conquering beauty's boasted charms,
With niveous breast and cheek of roseate hue,
Attempts the muse to sing.   No pleasing task
Awaits her early flight, no future fame
Indulgent hope anticipates, for soon
(The records of eternal wisdom say)

B

The subject of her song shall be no more.
Ambitious only to be known the last
Whose single voice, tho' dissonant, is rais'd,
Loudly to execrate infernal war,
Systems of murder and campaigns of blood.

Come, flaming Hecla! on thy adure brow,
Or near thy summit, Etna, let me stand;
While fumid clouds obnoxious roll around,
While streams of liquid fire in rage descend,
Sulphureous vapours vex the ambient air,
And showers of candent rocks informous fly
On every side: on every side Despair,
Tottering with phrenzy'd fear, shudders aghast
At Nature's elemental warfare wild!
What scene on earth so suited to inspire
Some faint impressions of that hellish strife,
By human tyrants foster'd; cursed War
With all its horrors, famine, fire, and blood,
Chill penury, and pestilential pains,

Languid disease, and maimed ghosts of men,
And every ill humanity deplores,
And every pang mortality can feel.

Infernal union ! who of these would sing
But that the suffering race of man may learn,
By past experience, and repeated charge,
To shun the monsters who dare patronize
Their conquests : sordid parasites and slaves,
Abject inglorious slaves, to murder bred ;
Statesmen corrupt, and superstitious priests,
Who mock mankind with surd and slavish creeds,
Sure cause of endless feuds, rebellions, party strife,
Driving from nations candid charity,
From families domestic peace and joy,
Each social comfort and each happy hour.

Look now beyond the birth of infant time,
Where Eden's bard, with flight sublimely bold,
Exulting sang of Chaos and of Heaven ;

Of deeds divine, and of thy monstrous birth,
Malefic War, of rebel angels born :
Thy burning phrenzy, and wide wasting ire,
By him depicted, rages in the mind
As erst in Heaven, ambition's chief delight
Thy foul distorted form disorder spread
ng empyreal hosts; and since on earth,
Where stands the city but has felt thy rage?
In what lone isle, rich vale, or barren waste,
Have not thy riches blaz'd, thy horrors reign'd?
Thy hungry maw sarcophagous devours
The sons of health; and pity's voice unknown,
Remorse stings not, and reason pleads in vain :
Humanity remonstrates, justice frowns,
And all in vain : insensate is thy breast;
The widow's anguish and the orphan's tear,
The feeble intercessions of old age,
The modest eloquence of virgin beauty,
With brutal scorn, with savage violence,
Rejected. O frail man, self-doating man!

Where is thy virile independance? all
Imaginary boasting.   Here peruse
(And blush at thy pretensions) the foul page
Of thy ancestral lineage; there behold
Historic truths unfold the blackest deeds,
When individuals of thy equal race,
Usurping wide dominion, regal power,
Imperious issue insolent commands;
And force from every tongue, and every heart,
Implicit homage, and obedience vile.
No sacred haunt of virtue or of learning,
Of wedded love, or virgin chastity,
Could e'er protect from the lascivious eye
And parsimonious grasp of tyrant power.
What forms the bulky annals of the earth
But War's exploits! What few events occur
That feast the philosophic mind, or please
The bounteous and humane? How seldom shines
The sun of peace, of concord, or of joy?

O mistress of the inexperienc'd world,
Imperious Babylon, thy actions rise
Conspicuous, and thy boasted strength displays
Thy lofty eminence and tyrant sway,
The scourge of nations : Wars unjust and base,
Detested precedents of pride and rage,
Pollute thy local annals; forth from thee
Stalks ever grim oppression, and his frown
Blights every bliss; the lightning of his eye
Makes desolate the provinces, and crimes,
Unnatural and inhuman, mark his way
Sanguifluous.   But not in Heaven unheard
Thy victim's agonies and dying groans,
Nor long unpunish'd; wild destruction comes
Abrupt, when midnight revelry reclines
On the lewd lap of pamper'd luxury ;
Vengeance awakes ! nocturnal carnage sharps
His thirsty glave, and drunkards reel to death !
Cyrus, prophetic hero, seal'd thy doom,

He level'd all thy lofty battlements,
Tumbling to heaps of undistinguish'd dust,
Thy walls bituminous, thy ponderous towers,
And all thy mighty magazines of war:
' As thou hast done, so shall be done to thee * ;'
Thou hast in blood and wanton cruelty
Laid desolate the cities of the earth
With dreadful devastation, and thy crimes
Shall now recoil on thy polluted head
With tenfold rage : no more in thee is heard
The festive mirth of jocund merriment ;
Princes enthron'd in thee no more receive
The laud of venal tongues; thy power and pride,
In one portentous hour, for ever gone.

Where shall the eye, that weeps at human woe,
Find the historic page without a tear ?
Descending thro' the maze of time, behold
What awful revolutions roll around ;

* Jeremiah, 50—xv.

Opinions various start on every side,
New creeds of faith, new codes of human laws,
Crowd on each other, and each novel change,
Prelude of bloody slaughter, war, and death.

Persian simplicity soon disappears,
And peace and harmony with mutual tears
Follow her honest steps; voluptuous sloth
Creeps o'er the land and enervates each arm;
Nurs'd in the Aulic cabinet, vain pride
Spreads her fantastic brood, taught to proclaim
Decrees altisonant and laws unjust.

How thy weak millions boast when a proud prince*
Affects the God without the creature's skill.
Impious autocracy! that dare presume
To claim supernal honours, only due
To Heaven's omnipotent eternal king!
Evanid dynasty! for soon he comes,

* Xerxes.

Darius, last of all thy gaudy race;
Two centuries had scarce beheld the pomp
Of three united kingdoms blaze in gold,
But all the vast magnificence and wealth,
Sequent on pride and absolute command,
Must own a conqueror : behold, * he comes
In all the dreadful discipline, War
Infuriate ; youthful ardour in his eye ;
Ambition swells his breast armipotent ;
And laurels, dipt in floods of human gore,
Adorn his brow ! Low on the earth Persia
Immartial lies : so falls, so fades the glare
Of sublunary grandeur ! Fame has left
Long since thy igneous regions, arid now
And scarcely known to geographic pen :
Lost in the labyrinth of implex date,
Thy sanguine history only can afford
Events of blood, as princes rose and fell,
Or superstition, pamper'd with the spoils
Of cruel War, triumph'd o'er peace and man.

* Alexander.

Here then, reflection, ask the busy world
To pause, and meditate on Persia's doom.
Experience! O! how dearly art thou bought,
If tides of human blood must flow in vain!
Had Peace, within her amaranthine bower,
Unceasing sang, what millions had her reign
Preserv'd from famine, flame, and murdering steel!

No wide extended wastes should then reproach
The wants of indolence; no moss-grown ruins,
Or level'd battlements, rehearse the crimes
Of contumacious War: nor cities vast
Where commerce pour'd her stores from every
        clime,
Where dædal industry, with clangous art
Inventive, all the wants of life supplied;
Should not as now in horrent desolation
Imbrute the memory of early days,
Or mourn the wrongs of independant man.
O Time, what wonders have thy eyes beheld!
The crowded city lost in exhalations.

Whose name celebrious aw'd the wondering world,
And forth from every gate battailous pour'd
Unnumbered warriors to the field of blood;
Waste and abandoned, yonder look it lies!
The foul resort of reptiles venomous,
And every hateful bird: but seldom found
By philosophic travellers, but seldom wept
In the poetic page.　Forbid it, Heaven,
That e'er Britannia's sons, by wars unjust,
Voluptuous apathy, or vice corrupt,
Should ere deserve so dread, so just a doom!

But see the victor Macedonian chief,
In all the wild delirium of success,
Stride o'er the nations! What vindictive rage
Now swells his veins? Is this ambitious fire?
Are these the exploits of glory; these the sports
Of youthful courage, or the enraged ire
Of foul incarnate fiends? What can demand,
What can excuse this waste of human blood?

Shall one aspiring tyrant, void of fear,
Impugn the peace of nations, and destroy
The sedulous employment of an age
In one terrific hour? Audacious chief!
To worry nature with the dogs of war,
Hurl devastation o'er the affrighted globe,
And brave the vengeance of a suffering world!
Awake, O pity! wake thee fell revenge!
Brandish thy thirsty poniard, pierce his heart!
Drink, drink his boiling blood! and drive his soul
To howl its vengeance in the realms below!

Endless the task to tell of every fiend
Who, bursting all the bonds of equity,
Sprung with rapacious talons on the poor,
Devouring every comfort, every joy!

High on the everlasting hills of fame,
Sublime, majestic, tread the sons of Greece;
The sage historian, the laurel'd bard,

The patriot brave, who for his country. bled,
As thou, Leonidas of Spartan soul,
Thine was the race of glory! thy career,
Emerging brilliant from the wrecks of time,
Outshines the wisdom of a thousand years!
Wars, such as thine, stern justice will defend;
And tho' humanity averts her eye
From scenes of blood, she spares, she pities *thee*,
Admires thy virtues, and deplores thy fate.
But e'en thy country, where firm patriots rose
As constellations eminently bright,
Must fall. War triumphs! eloquence nor art,
Nor disciplin'd severity, nor all
The rigid sapience of the heathen world,
Could bar the progress of venality;
Whose venine draught enerves the patriot's soul,
Creeps with ignoble stealth thro' every rank
Of social life; tempts the low sordid mind
Of griping avarice with shining dust;
Provokes the passions of the aspiring youth

With sweet utopian dreams of boundless power:
Then Envy stares, and Discord springs to life
Wild as the forest wolf! ferocious War
Mounts his iron chariot.   Unhappy Greece!
Must thou too fall beneath his brazen wheels,
Thy artuous generations lie supine,
Prostrate, submissive at the conqueror's feet?
Shent all thy plans of legislative lore,
Virtuous amaritude, and patriot zeal:
Thy sculptor'd fanes, where many a weary arm
With simultaneous strength, industrious spent
All the robust and lively hours of life;
To adorn the massy architrave, and rear
The chissel'd arcade, Doric and Tuscan,
Salon and Corridor, infrangible;
The echoing dome and cornic'd pedestal,
Reserv'd for genius to occupate;
Illustrious eminence! while ages roll,
Mankind with admiration may behold
And learn to imitate exalted worth:

These are no more.—Not the rude hand of time,
Nor elemental furor, could erode
The ponderous monuments of human skill;
'Twas the more stubborn rage of ferine man,
Uprais'd the effraiable gonfalon of war
With harsh outrageous detonation;
Ming.ing eternal tumult.   Wreck on wreck!
Temples immane, and amphitheatres vast,
Dight mausoleums, sinuous aqueducts,
And all the pride, and all the pomp of Greece,
Fell War dilapidates: Her archives lost,
Her sons dispers'd, fair science takes her flight;
Barbaric darkness, hovers o'er the land,
A mental night! and Greece is now no more!

　　Now see, advancing from the lutulent shores
Of the wide spreading Nile, thro' Afric sands,
A mixed multitude from bondage base
And slavish yokes exonerate; the charge
Of heavenly wisdom and almighty power.

Long had oppression's adamantine chain,
Bow'd down in ignominious servitude,
The patriarch Abraham's inconstant race;
Long had Egyptian cruelty compell'd
To office menial, and toil severe;
Beneath keen stripes and mercilefs commands,
To raise the everlasting pyramid !
And delve the fubterraneous catacomb !
Where kingly carcases may lie fecure
From the sharp fangs of deleterious time;
To daze the visual sense of unborn men.
But heaven's eternal Deity look'd down
With high disdain on th' ambitious views
Of haughty monarchs: sovereign pity, such
As mortals cannot comprehend, then sway'd
Th' Almighty's breast; and then, to fulfil
The patriarchal covenant, display'd
His mighty power in acts miraculous;
When rattling hail and livid lightnings mix,
And lurid darknefs in chaotic night

Involves the face of nature : Blains and boils,
And pestilential plagues, and vermin vile,
And loathed reptiles, numberless, devour
Creation's vegetative robe; and who,
Begirt in regal pomp, or clasp'd in power,
(As erst chilvaric knight in armature)
Can e'er withstand th' Omnipotence of heaven?

Shall the vain tyrant, that with impious front
Stoops to adore a deity of gold,
That drives the untaught of his kindred race
Unjustly to the brink of human life,
To linger on the shivering algid socks
Of barren poverty; hears not the groans
Of hoary age, nor bends his haughty eye
On grief forlorn, or skeletons of woe;
That sports with death, and renders the dank grave
An envy'd palace where the weary rest;
Shall crimes like these escape the wrath of heaven?
Behold what punishment is in reserve

c

For unrelenting despots; and what care,
What providential vigilance appears,
For suffering virtue and oppressed worth.
With marvellous phenomenon the clouds,
Condens'd as pillars architectural,
A van impregnable presents by day,
By night a spiry flame of sacred fire,
Forth from the jaws of tyranny to lead
A weak defencelefs nation. Nature obeys
The mandates of the man by heaven inspir'd;
The astonish'd deep recoils, in wild amaze
Upturns innumerable waves commixt,
Impellent wave on wave emerging pour
Rapid succession, till the affrighted earth
From the creation bury'd 'neath the abysm
Unfathomable of floods tempestuous,
Beheld the solar blaze: Then Abraham's race,
The multifarious colony of heaven,
Path'd o'er the untrodden rocks. Elate with
Vain presumptuous confidence, the host

Of Egypt follow'd ; prone 'twixt the parted gurge,
With fatal emulation horsemen throng,
In all the dread habiliments of war;
Cohorts on foot, and scythed chariots :
When, lo! the sever'd surges instant close,
Rushing impetuous o'er the frantic host;
Gulph'd in the choaking flood the warriors sink,
Loud uttering inarticulate shrieks,
And lamentable screams of horror; such
As earth had never heard.   Condign, severe
Their dreadful fate; just, for no corporal pains
Could e'er to pity move their harden'd hearts,
No meek submission satisfy their pride,
Or bate the rigour of their harsh commands.
Now thro' the sultry desert, vast and wide,
With weary steps they pace the parched sands,
While adure Siroc * flings his hottest glow,
And factious whirlwinds grind the unarm'd earth
To clouds of volant dust.   Onward they track

* South-east wind.

C 2

The desolate regions, oft at utmost need
Preserv'd from perilous mischance; tho' loud
The murmurings of ingratitude, and stout
Rebellion rears his proud seditious crest.
Still kind and merciful the Eternal arm
Subdues the opposing nations: pardons all
The violations of his sacred law,
And with long suffering wears the affranchis'd tribes
Down to the tomb.   More blest their sons,
And more deserving of the promised land.
That land, whose sordid aborigines, lost
To every virtuous excellence, dare boast
Of the most foul and filthy vices, such
As man should never name without a glow
Of inward loathing and warm indignation.
These to extirp the Israelites were sent;
That their flagitious crimes may not extend
Thro' the whole earth: Not brac'd in steel,
Nor train'd to murderous discipline severe;
So human strength had claim'd the conqueror's
    meed:

But gradient careless to the brazen gates
Of hostile cities, whose high ponderous walls,
And collossean towers, might laugh to scorn
The angry menaces of abler arms;
But that within dwelt foul nefarious vice;
Impotent sloth, and nerveless luxury:
These to annihilate, was heaven's command,
Guilt flies and vengeance follows, bloody War
Prowls with vindictive fury thro' the land!
O'erturns the nemoral gods, whose stupid priests,
Rapt'd in mad orgies, with unsparing hand
Excarnate their own limbs.   Defence is vain,
For Heaven itself with irresistless wrath
Pours down destruction on the flying foe * :
Nor mountain wilds, nor desert solitudes,
Nor pathless woods, nor cavern'd rocks, afford
Safe shelter in the final suffering day
Of retribution.   Yet not these, nor all

* Joshua x. 11.

The visitations of a chastening God,
Could awe to meek submission, or restrain
From gross idolatry, the stubborn race
By such all-powerful wisdom freed and led
Incipient from the bonds of servitude,
And dreary Arab wastes, to fructuous lands,
Where virent Spring, array'd in rural flowers,
Leads round the jocund seasons: fruits and herbs,
Ultroneous, deck the valleys, and adorn
The aspiring hills; while skipping flocks and herds
Innumerable deck the fertile fields.
Unthinking and incorrigible race,
So soon to lose remembrance of that power
Who gave them life, and then fair liberty;
So soon to stoop insensate to the base
Of carved statues, and rude images
Of clay-formed gods; so soon to imitate
The execrable crimes of Pagan guilt;
Heedless of all the sanative advice
Of Heaven-directed Judges, or the calls

Of inspirated prophets.   Their vigour fled!
Lost to the fortitude invincible
Of animating liberty, to yield
To one frail man those inborn sacred rights,
Which death alone should sever from the heart.
Soon come the bitter days of keen regret,
When by experience sorely were they taught
Unlimited obedience was unjust:
When, 'stablish'd in some rich luxuriant vale,
Compas'd with cares domestic, and the joys
A father and a husband can possess,
While labouring cheerful at his daily toil,
Sudden resounding from contiguous hills,
Echoes the clangous trumpet's hostile blast!
Down drops the pruning hook—aghast he st...!
Revolving all the miseries of mischance
In fickle War !—beholds his distant cot
With inward anguish: the tear paternal
Streams down his manly cheek. Homeward he turns
With slow and solitary steps; and there

The dreadful sounds had rais'd virtuous alarms
And apprehensive fears : Again the sounds
Vibrate harsh discord! Now, farewell he cries—
For I am not my own.—And then, dissolv'd
In tenderness and love, the throbbing breast
Sobs forth such language tongues can never tell.

Time flies, and monarchs as swift meteors reign :
But few thy virtuous chiefs, but few thy days
Of tranquil peace.   See grim Murder scowls!
Assassination stalks at highest noon
With brandish'd dagger! Dark Conspiracy
Broods death and vengeance in the murky night!
His crimson streamer dauntless Treason rears;
And bold Rebellion-lights the torch of War.
Then comes the wreck of happiness ! Then comes
The expiring groans of civil government :
When foreign foes invade, and party strife
Employs the youthful sword, what then can save ?
Not individual valour, tho' the arm

Of Manhoa's son in hostile wrath had ris'n;
Nor worth, nor wisdom, sage, nor saint divine.
The foe strides on invincible in might,
Jerusalem and all her bulwarks blaze!
The flaming firebrand seeks the holy gate,
And ponderous engines shake the mighty walls
Of that stupendous fane, where God himself
Display'd to mortal eyes his glories bright:
Amidst the rancour indiscriminate
Of equalizing war, the portals blaze!
The pillars drop! the crashing cedars fall!
The sacred altar smokes with human gore!
The dread finale a biped holocaust!
The awful oratory's veil'd recess,
Which the unhallow'd feet of fraud had trod,
And base hypocrisy had long defil'd,
The raging element incinerates.
To every lofty pile and habitation
The conflagration spreads, but language fails,
Imagination only can depict

The dreadful horrors of that feral hour,
When wak'd to madness all the passions rage
Unutterable! Despair, and fear, and hate,
Paternal love, remorse, and fierce revenge,
Distorts each countenance, distracts each mind;
Aloft the Painim's banner conquering flies
O'er Palestina's cities: Vale and plain,
And subterrany holds, and antres dire,
Reverberate the howlings of despair.   •
Dragg'd unrelentless from the fruitful field,
The simple peasant, and the rustic swain,
Are forc'd from home and happiness away,
To people distant regions: slaves to War,
The monster goads them on without a tear;
Bending beneath a load of galling chains,
To serve, as erst in Egypt's steril lands,
A thousand petty tyrants.   Sad reverse
Of former splendid triumphs; hear their strains,
Their melancholy strains of plaintive woe,
Wak'd by the heart-felt sorrow memory gives;

When recollection, wandering o'er the scenes
Of grandeur past, with retrospective glance,
Hangs fondly on the halcyon transient hours
When youth, carousing in the arms of hope,
Tripp'd o'er her gay interminable plain.
But weary nature checks the utopian bliss,
And back to hopeless slavery calls the mind:
Facinorous circumstance of savage war!
O state forlorn, that ever god-like man
Should stoop to slavery ! to cringe, and fawn,
To tremble at a fellow-mortal's frown,
Nor strength, nor time, nor life at his command!

Again, when contrite penitence sincere,
Glows in the captive's breast, the judge of heaven
Pardons the sins of contumacious man:
Rescues again from ignominious bonds;
Again restores to liberty, and scenes
Only familiar to the rheumy eyes
Of hoar senectude. Fraternal fetters now

Unite the wandering race; the bonds of love
And unanimity confine more sure
The agency of man, than all the chains
Despots can forge, or fortitude sustain.
With grateful hearts to Sion's sacred mount,
The blended tribes pursue their destin'd way:
But few return'd, whose eyes had ere beheld
Their country's glory, living now to weep
Her barren state, and foul dishonour'd name.
What fond emotions, joy, and sharp regret,
Must then invade the breast of every sire,
When for their much-lov'd city's circling walls
Brambles abrupt, and rude impervious heaps
Of stony ruins rise? The elders point
Where the great Temple stood; rehearsing all
Their national successes when their tribes
Faithfully serv'd the ever-living God:
And how, when polytheism altars rais'd
In every rural boscade; then at once
Triumph'd their despicable foes, and then

The warrior's prowess fled, courage amort,
And every vigorous arm quickly became
Debile and impotent:—then warmly urg'd,
How needful for their own prosperity,
To keep their pure religion undefil'd:
To cultivate the social arts of peace;
Refrain from civil broils, and proud demean,
That vast unweildy domination knew
But little peace: that national content
Could only live with equitable laws:
That justice only should be absolute
In power and influence: that experience past
Must learn them one important useful truth—
That nations in this world are punish'd
For public crimes, and base notorious guilt.

With indefatigable zeal the tribes
Rebuild their desolated fanes; again
Uprear the circling walls and stately tow'rs.
Alas! only rebuilt to grace a conqu'ror's reign;

For see, the universal murd'rer * comes,
Forcing subjection unconditional :
And following him, the Syrian monarchs claim
Homage and annual tribute; these divide
The oppressed land, now no longer known
By title ancestral, nor longer fear'd
By states conterminous; hated, despis'd,
Haras'd,depress'd,reproach'd, and laugh'd to scorn.

And yet another retributive storm
Impet'ous comes; in Egypt's † sultry plains
The dreadful whirlwind rises; on it scowls,
Nigrescent, to the feeble trembling gates
Of David's royal city.   Ten thousand slain,
And twice ten thousand dragg'd to servitude,
The half dispeopled provinces pour forth
Horrible outcries, lorn and defenceless.
Soon a louder hurricane minacious, roars

---

* Alexander.   † Invasion of Ptolemeus Lagi.

Dreadful denunciations; the Syrian fiend*,

(For sure no human mind could ere inflict

Such execrable punishments) unfurls

His bloody banners on the Temple's top,

While sacrilegious plunderers prey within,

While thro' the yelling streets fell Massacre

Riots in gore; Torture triumphant howls

Malicious fury, while he elevates

His lofty scaffold; inexorably rears

His racking engines and his torturing wheels.

Yet from this horrid scene of blood and death,

Once more the Jews to independence rise,

When Mattathias and his warlike sons

Subdu'd the pagan despots, and regain'd

Their country's freedom: soon the flame expires.

Roman ambition strides around the world,

Raging like fires volcanic, or vast seas

From mounded dikes broke loose, that swallow up

* Antiochus Epiphanes.

Creation's vary'd progeny: so rag'd the ire
Of Roman legions, when by Pompey led,
Thro' Asian climes to Palestina's land.
In vain the Israelites bar up their gates
To oppose their fierce invaders: soon they yield,
And everlasting bondage is their lot.

And now the solemn, the eventful hour
Draws nigh, when the last summons calls
To national repentance.—He comes!—
The prince of peace, the great Messiah comes!
Strike every chord of harmony and love,
Join every land! Ye bards of Greece and Rome,
Why sleep your lyres? to you and all your sons,
The great important promises extend!
No more, ye Athenian sciolists, no more
Ye oriental sages, boast no more
Polemic wisdom: now the eye has seen,
'Tis true! the dubious hop'd-for point is true,
There is!—there is a life beyond the grave.

Spring from your slothful shades, ye Afric swains;
Rise Asiatics, from your banquets rise;
And rouse *thee*, barbarous Europe, from thy Wars;
Shake off these futile feuds, and learn to live
As mortals worthy of immortal life.
But first, ye Jews, burst forth the loud acclaim;
Your holy Prophet lives, your Saviour reigns!
From age to age foretold, and now confirm'd
By ev'ry circumstance of time and place.
Endow'd with supernatural powers, and these
Exercent in your streets; abolish then
Your ceremonious code and mystic rites,
For, lo! the prescient Archetype is come!
What greater honour than to learn of him
The ways of peace and everlasting life?
Why lingers your belief, expect you still
A temporal prince and wide extensive rule?
O senseless race! that cannot wisdom learn
Of sage experience.   Than whips and chains,
Calamitous captivities, and Wars,

Are insufficient to instruct, how vain
Are sublunary hopes and worldly joys?
Come drown, in tears of grateful penitence,
Your factious enmities and party schisms.

Ah! barbarous vaticides! hell-breathing fiends!
What mean these dread convulsions? What por-
        tend
These agonies of nature? O, why hides
The orb of light, indignantly, his face
At highest noon? 'Tis your abhorred crimes
At which the whole creation groans!—'Tis past!
In vain the dumb proclaim'd his power divine
In loud rejoicings, and the eternal God,
From heaven's high arches, testify'd of him:
Rejected,—scorn'd,—and crucify'd!—
Impious heretics! tho' promise made
(Should pure contrition purge the guilty breast)
Of pleasures immarcessible, in worlds
Of future glory and perennial joy.

Such truths promulg'd, by miracles confirm'd,
Might well lay claim to universal faith:
But prejudice incredulous puts on
His thickest mail, nor feels the mighty blows
Of heav'nly truth; and stubborn pride,
Deaf as the Pagan's God, with angry frown
Rejects celestial mercies.   Now farewel
To all the halcyon pleasures of sweet peace.
Asunder burst the bonds of social love,
Public prosperity, and private bliss;
Sedition roars a thousand accusations,
With rancour indiscriminate and base;
Slander, with venine tongue loquacious, pours
Volumes of angry words and bitter spleen;
These rising to unconquerable rage,
Unsheath the two-edg'd sword of civil war.
Then widows weep, and anarchs call to arms;
Fanatics prophesy, enthusiasts pray;
At once ascend to Heaven vehement calls
For vengeance and for mercy; the screams

Of suffering innocence, the groans of guilt.
Confiding yet in firm lapideous towers,
In mural strength, and military skill,
The infatuated race with rage defy
(Expecting aid miraculous) the power
Of mighty Rome.   And now thy dreadful doom,
Jerusalem, inevitably comes.
Hark! 'tis the din of arms,—bar up your gates,
Case up your fragile frames in plates of steel;
Ye bold cuirassiers wing the darts of death!
Haste thee, lymphatic zeal, thy country calls:
Fly superstition from thy gloomy shrine,
Behold what warlike hosts intrench thee round;
Up to your battlements, and see if now
Omnipotence again will condescend
To drive your fierce invaders from their camp.
No, 'tis the final triumph of fell War,
Valiant resistance only points to death:
Courage can only with revenge expire.
Who can behold with firm and dauntless gaze

Gigantic famine rave along thy streets?
Who can with nerves compos'd, and steady arm,
Defy the dreadful orgasm of his might?
Patience and fortitude, with active steps,
Run trembling from the terrors of his mien:
To appease the frantic fury of his tongue,
Fathers with rage demoniac rive the hearts
Of their own offspring!—Israel, where's thy God?
See! see! thy strong, thy tripple barrier falls!
Thronging thro' wide embrasures rush thy foes:
Thro' every street the curling flame extends,
A vast volcano! rolling to the heavens
(As once Gomorrah) sheets of angry fire!

Thus fell Jerusalem! at once the scorn
And terror of the world; driven from their homes,
The wretched few whom Providence preserv'd,
Wander as vagrants now thro' every land—
A dread example to the human race,

What punishment depravity deserves,
What great calamities fierce War inflicts!

But see yon infant state arise to fame;
Sprung from the itinerant and war-worn race
Who fled the wreck of Troy's ill fated walls,
And ravish'd Sabines: nurs'd, as fame reports,
By savage quadruped; prognostic dire
Of worse than canine rage! The earliest art
A rising nation cultivates (O shame,
For ever hide such arts from human skill)
Must be the art of War! and Rome, to thee,
To thee belongs such unexampled guilt!
How arrogant is gay prosperity,
And how assuming conquest! Rome's success
Was Rome's destruction! Insatiate War,
With never-ceasing howl, demands more blood,
Ambition more dominion! Monsters both,
That scorn all laws, contemn all just restraint,

Whose firm adherents, heedless of the ills
That fall on patience and on poverty,
With mad precipitation, equal rage,
Rush on the bold invaders of their rights,
And peaceful nations.   How severely wise
Should be that man, to whom a country trusts
The management of murder! Oft was Rome
By her own armies conquer'd; mighty power
Transforms the patriot to the oppressor!
As numbers swell'd the new Idalian state,
Her pride increas'd; defenders of her weal
Became savage brigands, who turn'd their arms
Where'er the prospect of success led on
Their sanguine hopes; tho' many a time reprov'd
By valour and by virtue.   *Pyrrhus* came
Well skill'd in arms, with stately walking tow'rs,
And Grecian phalanx, to abate their pride.
And following him the Alpine hero * taught,

* Hannibal.

Success was never certain : say, proud Rome,
Was it true glory, was it honour's plan,
To hire assassins to revenge thy blood,
And hunt an aged warrior round the world ?
Ignoble conquerors ! such plagues await
Your boasted city as your arms impos'd
When Carthage, Corinth, and Numantia fell !
In thy black catalogue of governors,
By fraud, or force, or vile corruption made;
In vain the friend of man seeks for a soul
Congenial with his own.   Thy tyrants serve
As models for the proud of every age;
Teaching ambition how he may arise
To earthly dignities, by fawning arts
And flattering promises; and when secure,
The acme of his power spurns the mean slaves
Whose valour carv'd his way: narcotic draughts,
From wanton pleasure's chalice, steels the heart
Against the calls of nature; scenes of blood,
And fields of slaughter, force no tears from him;

But ah! beware, ye copyists of their crimes,
Think how the tyrants fell! and learn, O man!
How frail thy nature. Rome's rapacious sons,
Accustom'd long to conquest, never paus'd
To muse on dark futurity's designs.
Attir'd in glittering robes, corruption stood,
Commanding universal adoration;
Plebeians, senators, and monarchs, fall
Before the magic idol—and with them fell
The dignities of Rome. Regions too vast
For justice at one view to comprehend:
Oppressed districts rise at every call
To claim their rights, when base perfidious men,
With show of pleasing virtues, lead them on
To desperate warfare. Soon the state becomes
One mighty ocean of contending storms;
In every province factious tumults rise,
While from the eternal snows of frozen climes,
Numberless hordes of fierce barbarians pour,
As swarms of hungry locusts. Following them,

Forth from the Caspian shores, the savage Huns,
And Alans bold, in countless myriads rush,
As rav'nous tygers o'er the fertile fields
Of European plains.   Time had not seen,
In all his revolutions, scenes like these;
Grim death till now was never satisfied,
War never glutted: Imagination
Sickens at the sight; what Gothic fury spar'd
The Vandal Chief * devours, and Rome expires
In horrible convulsions.   Thus comes thy fate,
From rude benighted corners of the world,
Where thy vindictive ire had never rang'd
For base manubial plunder: thus then comes
That punishment the Almighty still reserves
For mean licentious vice and high ambition.

Now languish'd learning, and the social arts.
Dark years of supertsition lost the lore

---

* Gesneric.

Of Greek philosophers; but still retain'd
The murdering arts of War, each idal lord
By slow encroachments arrogates his power;
Battling his stoutest vassals on the plains,
As thirst of conquest, or as fierce revenge,
Inflam'd his breast.   The clouded years roll on,
When the mad prophet * blew the trump of War,
Gathering the scatter'd nations all to arms;
Declaring pure and everlasting joys
Awaited him who in his battles fell.
Then with such cogent reasons urg'd his creed,
Such irresistless arguments †, that man
Attempts not opposition; till blind zeal,
With blood as hot, and crimes as black as theirs,
Calls up his bigot untaught followers ‡ :
Then frantic emigrants, from every state
Europa owns, file to the hostile fields,
With all that rage infernal War provokes,

* Mahomet.   † Fire and sword.   ‡ Crusades.

When superstition whets the sanguine sword!
Good chri███ murd'rers, that with pious tongues
Loudly exclaim'd against the Saracens,
And their fanatic conquests; now rush on
To warfare, wild and barbarous as them.
Ah! what an endless scroll of uncouth names,
Famous for skill in arms and bold emprise,
The pompous age of chivalry presents,
Where fiction loves to rove; recounting tales
Romantic of bold knights and virgins fair,
By wizard's art, and talismanic power,
And dragon's vigilance, in castles pent,
Forlorn and weeping for some hidden cares,
As love-sick melancholy, mop'd and sad;
When lo, some civil, brave, advent'rer comes,
With vig'rous neighing steed, and nodding crest,
With pond'rous lance, and egis ever bright,
Achieving wonderful exploits of strength,
Magicians, hydras, spells, enchantments, all
Dissolve as airy bubbles!—Happy world,

If never actions worse than these disgrac'd
Thy narratives of slaughter.—See the East
Delug'd in blood! Turkmans and Tartars joi..
Ferocious combat, and the nations dread
Total extinction, when their savage chiefs
Deluge the world with floods of human gore.
Orchanes, Bajazet, and *Tamerlane,*
And he the conqueror of Trebizond *,
The Tartar *Gingis,* and bold *Nadir Kan:*
Why live their actions in the historic page,
Unless for execration? Patterns vile!
What fearful monsters are ambitious men,
When unrestrain'd by salutary laws?
What pen can tell Iberia's heavy woes,
When the revengeful Moors invade her coasts;
Or Albion's state, when northern robbers † prey
Implacably; or Saxon traitors gend
Intern commotions. Yet in these rude days
Ignorance affords some plea for frequent Wars,

* Mahomet II.   † Scots and Picts.

Weak superstition may apologize
For many crimes: but have mankind
Yet learn'd to live as brethren? yet resolv'd
To banish legal murder from the earth?—
Rising from Gothic darkness, science shines
Each rolling year with more resplendent light:
Invention roves exulting round the world,
Instructing nations in the useful arts:
And had the arts of peace alone employ'd
His studious hours, the happy race of man
Had never wept: or had humanity
In ev'ry breast, as in our *Bacon's* glow'd;
Arts that excite revenge, or stimulate
Ambitious projects, never had been known.
But 'twas for Monks * reserv'd to teach mankind
More expeditious murder!—And seldom fail'd
The holy mother church in breeding broils,
Wherein her pious advocates may learn

* Swartz of Cologn.

The novel arts.   Accursed homicides!
'Twas your hot bigotry, and bastard zeal,
So long in darkness hid the human mind,
Clouding the sky of reason with the storms
Of superstition's sombre hemisphere.
Inexorable foes of man and truth!
To you may War attribute half his ills,
And all his modern terrors.—Many a slave,
Expiring in the agonies of death,
Has breath'd his last anathemas on you:
Repenting sore that inauspicious day
He left his simple joys and native home,
To roam about the world an abject slave:
Bearing vile instruments of pain and death,
To level at the heads of unknown men.

Behold yon mangled bleeding body, borne
Forth from the field of death; but now his cheek
Glow'd with the bloom of health; but now his heart
Beat rapture to the soothing songs of hope,
Whose magic melody inspir'd his breast

With many a pleasing dream of days to come;
When all these dreadful scenes of blood should
     close,
And peace restore him to his rustic vale,
And loving relatives, and long lost friends.
Ah! but the sweet delusive sounds have ceas'd:
See how his body writhes with torturing pains!
Hear how he groans! while busy ruthless men
Probe his deep wounds, and amputate his limbs!
Now how revers'd the prospect of his life,
If life should be his lot; a ling'ring scene
Of pain and penury, of helpless health,
And vile dependance:—a frail and useless drone
In the great hive of men: or perhaps to rove
A vagous mendicant, by offals foul
And casual bounty fed! As men improv'd
In every science, War itself became
'A settled theory, by long practice brought
To great perfection: when Gallia's king *

* Charles VII.

(Eternal infamy hang o'er his name)
Completely organiz'd the art of War!
Maintaining mercenary bands of men
In constant service; disciplin'd, exact,
And ever ready to attend his nod,
Whether in just defence of nat'ral rights,
Or mad ambitious projects.   These to keep
In shining arms, and terrible attire,
The nation groans beneath the heavy load   ·
Of grievous imposts: and if murmurs rise,
The slaves they clothe on them let fall their ire
Unmerciful.   When Man's inur'd to arms,
And train'd in desperate murder's-school profane,
The social virtues all forsake his breast,
And all the furious passions rise to arms,
As heedless impulse calls; no prattling babes,
No tender wife, has he to rouse the fears
Of soft affection, or to chase the cares
Of solitary hours; no soothing home
To rest his weary limbs; no friend sincere,

E

To share his sorrows, and partake his joys,
(If joy that heart can feel, that feels not grief
And keen remorse, when memory calls to mind
The many mortals his vindictive arm
Has sent unpitied to the gloomy grave).
Alone, amidst the thousands of his kind,
Alike in circumstance, whose selfish souls
(Selfish, alas, from dire necessity)
Exchange no little marks of mutual love;
But each suspicious eye, with envious frown,
Seems to suspect his comrade feels more bliss,
Beholds more pleasure and content, than him.

Thus came a train of ills on every state,
And all the offspring of infernal War!
Princes no longer trust their subjects love;
No longer on their loyalty depend,
For meek obedience or sure protection.
See adverse interests now divide each state,
Struggling for freedom and prerogative.

The despot Louis * soon extends that power
His sire attain'd; aiming a fatal blow
At dove-like peace and manly liberty.
On him let fall the curse of every age!
For he first brib'd a nation's delegates
Basely to sell her interests!—he first made known,
In European states, corruption's power;
And each succeeding prince, encroaching still
On nature's rights and ancient privilege,
Became, as eastern monarch's, absolute,
Imposing taxes and declaring wars
On frivolous pretences.—Female caprice,
And regal folly, oft has plung'd the world
In desperate contests; continued now,
Long as inveterate malice held his spleen,
Or envy, or revenge, swell'd up the breast
Of haughty arrogance.   Dissolv'd in sloth,
Withheld by trembling fear, the nations lay

* Louis XI.

Irresolute and hopeless.   And when came
The bold reformers * of the Papal church,
Still on Europa's continent fair peace
Was seldom seen.   Stern prejudice alarm'd,
Snatch'd up his arms, and bellow'd out for War!
Crying aloud, " there wanted no reform !
" That such reforms were dang'rous innovations;
" That by reform, sedition only meant
" Total destruction to the establish'd form,
" And pious principles of cath'lic faith.".
Unus'd to reason or to argument,
(Tho' deck'd with all the flowers of eloquence)
The sons of bigotry refuse to hear,
But drunk with rage, call on the fiery fiend,
Mad Persecution ! He in vain assaults
The fortresses of truth : impregnable
To all the attacks of open war, and all
The artful stratagems of secret guile.

* Luther, Zuinglius, Melancthon, &c.

What then could persecution? Racks, and chains,
And torturing wheels, and iron instruments,
Fram'd to inflict tormenting agonies,
But mock th' inventors! Truth immaculate,
Disdains corporeal sufferings; and alone,
Appeals to sov'reign Reason's grand tribunal.

Yet from the wreck of superstitious creeds,
No certain light arose: no friendly star
To guide humanity the devious road
To universal peace. As years revolve,
War triumphs! and every warfare adds
Fresh horrors to his mien! And even *now*,
When science roams at large about the world,
When men would fain be thought exceeding wise,
And talk of reason, and religion too,
As though their hearts felt what their tongues re-
    peat,
E'en *now* the monster triumphs!—and yet proud
    man

Affects benevolence and soft compassion,
When every vale resounds the crimes of War!
When every city throng'd with warlike bands,
And fortified with bastions and redoubts,
And dreadful battery's, whose thund'ring breath
Out-roar Gibello, prove his claims are false!
While every ocean bears to every shore,
Loads of obnoxious minerals:—and every sea
Is ting'd with vestiges of human blood!
To mercy thy pretensions all are vain,
For every chronicle records thy guilt!
And every active courier brings some tale
Of fresh immanity! Away, then, you
Who boast his independent excellence,
His immaterial soul, and powers sublime!
Savour his actions of ethereal mould?
Or claim his virtues kindred with the skies?
Ah, no! he is as other animals,
The slave of habit, and the child of chance;
What education makes him, meek and mild,

Savage, morose, compassionate, or vain,
As circumstance or accident inclines
His wav'ring heart: what then can regulate
His wayward appetites, or what restrain
His energetic passions? What can teach
Frail man to govern and to know *himself?*
O! for some panacea that might heal
All public quarrels, and all private brawls;
Some universal grand establishment,
Not of religious creeds, but moral schools,   ,
Where all the rising race of man may learn
Their own importance in creation's tribe:
Where Virtue may instruct the tender mind
In all the axioms of equity,
The principles of justice, and the laws
Of honest legislation; where fair Truth,
And bland Humanity, may lead the heart
Insensibly to mild Religion's shrine;
Where sage Experience may explain the dark,
And seeming cruel plans of Providence.

Where all the sciences sublime may daze
His visive pow'rs, excite his strong desires,
Expand his intellects, and raise his soul
To heav'nly contemplations!—Superior then
To earthly evils, he may well disdain
The favours or the frowns of fortune: rich
In abject poverty; with patience stor'd—
By fortitude defended—by wisdom led—
He journeys on thro' life with little noise;
Regardless of the grandeur of the great,
The calls of superstition, or the joys
Licentious Pleasure promises—and when comes
His final dissolution, calm, serene,
He quits this sublunary sphere, and hopes
For everlasting life beyond the grave.

O! cherish the fair vision: Time *may* bring
Such happy days, when War no more shall range
Triumphant thro' the world; when man no more
Shall slay his fellow man, or make his flesh

An article of commerce. Haste, ye hours,
Bring with you ever-smiling Peace, that men
May trumpet forth her glorious jubilee,
Thro' every land on this terraqueous orb!
That every tribe and every tongue may join,
And shout one general anthem to her praise!
Illustrious epoch! Man devoid of fear,
Shall then embrace his fellow, then shall hail
A CITIZEN of EARTH, a FREEMAN of the WORLD!

ODES.

TO HOPE.

HARK! Hark! what strains divine
    Swell in the volent gale,
    And echo thro' the dale:
'Tis HOPE with her enchanting tongue,
  Muse, snatch thy lyre, and join her song;
High to the paths of fame her sounds aspire,
Kindling the lover's flame, the poet's fire.
    Melodious thrills her dulcet lay,
To realms of perfect bliss, to worlds of endless day!
    Youth wild with ecstasy, and gay as spring,
    As light'ning flies to hear her sing!
    Patience, the guardian of her lofty throne,
    Hearing pale Misery's feeble moan;
      Tapers the devious road,
      To her divine abode:

The trembling victims of heart-gnawing Care,
　　　Listen with ravish'd ear,
　　　And smile at ghastly Fear,
　　And once beholding her resplendent light,
　　Nor heed Affliction's lingering night,
Nor fear the savage howlings of Despair.

　　Hast thou not heard wan Poverty repine?
　　　Hast thou not seen the tumults of his breast,
　　When hunger, cold, and sickness, all combine,
　　　To vex his weary soul, and break his rest?
　　Beneath yon hovel's lorn penurious shade,
　　His wretched skeleton on earth was laid;
　　And void of pity, o'er his haggard form
　　Howling contempt sweeps the rude storm!
　　　Nor bellowing winds, nor gushing rain,
　　Hear his faint voice complain:
　　　But lo! he starts at thy elysian song,
　　　　Celestial Hope! thy magic shell,
　　　As the arcanum of some wizard's spell,
　　　　Stays the full tide misfortune rolls along.

So well thy sounds his miseries beguile,
He lifts his tearful eye, and learns to smile.

What time Hibernia's briny deep,
    Or the chill Baltic's dashing wave,
    By furious boreal tempests drave
High as the Alps, as Cohoe steep!
Sport with the patient seaman's skill;
    And now aloft on liquid mountains borne,
    His vessel reels, his cordage torn!
Now to the depths profound his bark is hurl'd,
    Envelop'd in a wat'ry world!
    Prudence and Courage stand aghast,
    While Danger rides upon the mast,
    And would the stoutest heart appal,
    But that sweet Hope is heard to call:
    And soon her syren voice is known,
    They strive, with efforts not their own;
    Less loud the rattling thunders roar,
    Less vain the billows lash the shore.

Thus human ills, and elemental rage,
The harmony of Hope can evermore assuage.

Full many a youth, to Fortune's smile unknown,
   Whose ardent breast the tender flame conceals,
Had not the lamp of Hope so cheerful shone,
   Had left his life and all its varied ills:
Drooping despondency had led his feet,
To Melancholy's dark and sullen seat;
Despair had clouded each succeeding day,
And Suicide had found an easy prey.

Upborne to deeds with love and glory crown'd,
   Superior to the shafts of Fate,
   With independent joys elate,
The Patriot's fervent wishes bound :
   He asks no boon of glittering show,
   Nor fears what envy base can do;
   He loves not empty vain parade,
   By pride and not by merit made;

His jealous caution, and his eager eye,
Appals Corruption's selfish votary :
  By Hope's vibrations he inspir'd,
    Indignant views Oppression's iron reign,
  And soon with all her ardour fir'd,
    Breaks from his iron chain !

But hence, ye mundane themes no more,
Far better Hope remains in store;
  O for the tuneful harp of *Jesse's* son,
Immortal psalmist ! thy celestial lyre
  Needs not the fabled streams of Helicon,
Its sacred raptures to inspire.
The Christian's Hope, that glorious mental sun!
That stream of bliss! whose waters ever run:
  Transcendant emanation of a God !
    What load of ills the world can give,
  What stroke of sharp Affliction's rod,
    Of thee the truly pious can bereave ?

O whither would the Muse aspire,
    Upled by thee,
Presumptive heir of immortality !
Scoff, infidels; the Christian's holy fire,
Impatient of his groveling earthly stay,
Swells o'er the prospects of eternal day;
    How far do thy most flighty hopes extend—
    To Wealth, and Fame, and Honour? soon
      they end;
While his surmounting every mortal joy,
Aspires to bliss, which time can ne'er destroy!

TO HUMILITY.

WHERE Nymph, with ever smiling face,
  Where shall I find thy humble bow'r?
In what solitary place
  Pass with thee the social hour?
Dost thou delight by limpid streams to stray,
  Where peaceful waters gently glide,
Where sweet campestral flow'rs bedeck the plain?
The fragrant bloom of May;
Where the sun-burnt rural swain
  Enjoys content, unknown to pomp and pride.

Yes, social Maid, I know thy soothing voice
  Suits well with Nature's rich luxuriant scene:
There no disgusting forms depose thy joys,
  Nor mock the visions of thy eye serene.
The Peasant's cot, where rustic plainness dwells,
To thy meek view a sculptor'd roof excels.

And oft at eve, when stars appear,
    And faintly glimmer in the distant sky;
I love to see thee lend a willing ear,
    To tales of sweet simplicity.
Or with conversant smile, relate
What joys Content and Innocence afford;
What cares perplex the great;
How dull and ceaseless ceremony tires;
And what false Honour too requires;
And how unblest the man that hides his golden
      hoard.

Still more enchanting does thy worth appear,
    Fair daughter of the sorrow-soothing smile,
With wealth, and power, and beauty in thy train:
    No other grace can then compare,
    Not even envious Slander dare defile!
    Ah! did the world but cherish thy esteem,
    Or only love it as they seem,
Not Genius should repine, nor Penury complain.

When sultry August's calid ray,
 Pours on the Peasant's fainting head,
Incessant toil prolongs the lingering day,
 And oft he thinks upon his lowly bed:
 O child of Nature, then in Ceres' field
 What comforts may thy votaries yield;
How may they wing the weary hours,
 What stores of rich content bestow;
Content! that as the vernal showers
 Shall make Hope flourish in the vale of woe.
 Instructed by their melody of tongue,
 Mild Affability shall wake her song,
  To soothe the helpless and forlorn,
Who suffer from the gripe of cruel scorn:
 And thou, sweet Nymph, shalt plead their
  cause;
 Bounteous Philanthropy shall shout applause;
And he who joins his voice may well secure
 The greatest earthly good—the blessings of the
  poor.

OLD AGE.

FROM twilight groves and ever-green retreats,
Amid Elysian vales, far from the scenes
    Where Vice and Folly reign,
    And Passion guides the storm:

Come, hoary Age, and lead me to thy cell
Serene, attended by the peaceful hours,
    And o'er my temples shed
    Thy frost and silver snows.

Far from the tumult of meridian joys,
From Discord's harsh terrific cry remote,
    Sweet Peace, with cherub mien,
    Resides thy bowers among:

And in thy chamber slumbers rosy Health,
On mossy couch reclin'd; while at thy porch
    Blythe Temperance keeps watch,
    And drives Disease away.

No fearful spectres haunt thy midnight hour,
No superstitious terrors break thy rest,
    Hope at thy pillow sits,
    And whispers golden dreams.

Thy festive board a sweet repast affords,
And at thy right-hand sits with roses crown'd,
    A never failing guest—
        Conviviality.

Hence, morbid Care and pale Anxiety,
Intemperance with face of lurid glow;
    Intrusive guests, begone!
    Oh! leave me to repose.

Come, rev'rend Age, and bring thy hairy gown;
Soft, let me seek thy awful solitudes,
　　Where Meditation sits,
　　And ceaseless sabbath keeps;

Or slowly pacing o'er the mountain's brow,
While countless dew-drops glitter gemmy bright,
　　Delightful task to cull
　　Each herb and springing flower.

By sage Experience led, thrice happy state!
Of second innocence with wisdom join'd,
　　And science still intent
　　To trim her fading lamp.

Haste, wintry Age, in furred mantle clad;
I love thy simple joys, thy sky serene,
　　I need thy calm repose,
　　And sweet tranquillity.

TO FORTITUDE.

To thee, when clamorous passions rise,
　When grim Misfortune rears his head,
When friends are false, when Reason flies,
　Or languid Sickness waits around my bed;
　　To thee unshaken power I call,
　Amidst the tumult of uncertain strife,
　The groans and struggles of this transient life;
　　And when beneath the stroke of Fate I fall,
Contending with corrupt Mortality,
Clasp'd in thy firm embraces let me die.

O tell me where on mortal ground,
Thy form inflexible is found?

Dost thou in fields of blood delight to stray?
Dost thou beside the ruffian soldier stand,
    And guide his faltering hand,
  When rose his fellow men to slay?
  Undaunted canst thou hear the horrid yell,
    The dying agonies that echo round,
    From many a mangled corse upon the ground,
While thundering cannons roar an hideous knell?

  Or rather, dost thou seek the sordid cot,
  Where meagre Want pines thro' the tiresome
      day?
  To chase away the gloomy ghost of care,
  Drive forth the grisly phantoms of despair,
    And stor'd with patience there delight to stay,
  And cheer with soothing songs his wretched lot.

  When base Ingratitude alarms
  The virtuous breast with unexpected woe,
  Hast thou no potent charms,
  No rich supplies of comfort to bestow?

Shall Fraud and Violence oppress the just,
   Shall Envy blast the laurels of the brave!
Oppression trample Freedom in the dust,
   And not thy arm exert itself to save?
Oh! give thy calm delights, thy tranquil rest,
To every suffering heart, to every sinking breast!

    Shall savage nations, wild and rude,
    Possess thy virtues, Fortitude?
    Unknown to silent quivering Fear,
    When tortures, racks, and fires appear!
    Shall sullen Ignorance presume
    To brave the terrors of the tomb,
And not the christian learn thy patient creed;
    And not the philosophic mind,
    Chaste, virtuous, and refin'd,
Deserve and cherish thy unfading meed?
Yes, 'tis within the virtuous breast,
   Thou art a constant willing guest,
     Tho' every evil of this life be thine,
      Disdaining to repine.

The loudest storm Adversity can roar,
    The keenest anguish Nature can endure,
Assault in vain, his soul can soar,
    To joys celestial and secure :
Possessing thy firm adamantine shield,
His heart can never faint, his soul can never yield!

TO THE SPRING OF 1795.

Muse of the Morning, wake thy lyre,
To Heaven's enthusiastic fire!
Smite sublime the loudest string;
Hail the birth of April's morn,
That comes the face of Nature to adorn;
With Flora's nymphs divinely sing.
Content from every shepherd's tongue
Shall aid the grand melodious song;
With vocal Harmony shall fill each grove,
And perfect every heart in gratitude and love.

Hither then thy music bring,
Salutiferous muse of Spring:
Impatient lingers every warbling pair,
Flora, to see thy beauteous bloom declare,
That Spring confest adorns each verdant mead;

With smiling eloquence to stand,
And scatter with a lib'ral hand,
O'er every meadow, every vale, and plain,
Innumerous traits of thy auspicious reign.

Darling of Nature's vocal choir,
Ambitious herald of the op'ning morn,
Whose matin solo, quavering in the sky,
Wakes the shrill sounding horn;
Whose skilful notes descending from on high,
Arouse the slumbering shepherd from his bed;
Do thou begin the oral song,
'Tis healthful Spring demands thy lay,
Nature's bounteous holiday;
Sweet Echo shall thy notes prolong,
Till every chorister shall catch the song:
Then sweeping o'er the lengthen'd plain,
Sweet Echo shall repeat again;
The bird of night, sweet Philomel,
Her soft, lone, warbling notes shall swell,

To propagate the grateful tale,
Reviving still with morn's reviving gale,
Till all the wide creation raise
Anthems of general joy, of universal praise!

Pursue with gladly skilful hand,
The sweet vibrations of thy theme;
But ah! see on that distant verging land,
A form, whose eye as lightnings gleam;
'Tis hated War!—Muse, drop thy lyre!
For no return of rosy Spring
Can tempt thy trembling voice to sing;
No smile of Summer can inspire,
While that discordant fiend appears,
To drown the wise and good in tears;
In vain may Flora's gentle reign,
With fragrant flowers bedeck the plain;
In vain benignant Ceres toil,
With plenty to enrich our soil,

While thy curs'd phrenzy, fiend of hell!
Infernal source of human woe!
The page of history shall swell,
With deeds reversing Nature's plan,
When first she form'd the creature Man;
Thou shalt not ever triumph so!
For tho' disease with faltering gait,
And palsy'd Famine on thee wait,
Tho' mad Ambition drive thy car,
Yet shalt thou perish, hateful War!
Yet shall the seeds of future prospects grow;
Prophetic Truth shall blaze around,
With joy the rolling year be crown'd;
Thou shalt expire in everlasting death!
Then, muse of Spring, prepare thy wreath;
For then! no hostile band shall ere controul
The heavenly breathings of thy soul;
For then! Mankind united brave and free,
Shall ever, ever, welcome thee;

Thy shower refrigerant shall repay
The horrors of the wintry day,
Till Time, exulting with his charge, shall bring
An endless Peace, an everlasting Spring!

INDEPENDENCE.

LOUD let the threat'ning tempest roar,
  And death and danger guide the storm,
    While billows lash the rocky shore,
    While thunders roll around,
    And lightnings blast the ground,
    And whelming cataracts pour.
  Thine, Independence, is the smiling form,
    Thine is the stedfast eye,
To view unmov'd these passions of the sky,
Leaning on Fortitude and sweet Serenity.

  Come, then, dear idol of the human heart,
  To me thy powerful energies impart;
    Then Fate let fly thy host of ills,—
    Contempt with scowling eye,
    Grim visag'd Poverty,

Disease with faltering gate,
And grinning Want, and everlasting Hate:
Arm'd with thy spirit let them rage,
The free-born soul shall mock their spite,
Disdainful of the wars they wage,
Shall gloriously retire within her native might.
Let parasites and tyrants frown,
And mad Ambition heave his massy lance,
Oppos'd to thy resistless glance,
How feebly drops it down!
How vain for such weak mortals of the earth,
E'er to contend with thee of heavenly birth.

Spirit of Independence! sacred flame!
And is it thine to prop the sinking soul,
That groans beneath Oppression's iron power,
Within whose dungeon Hope may never gleam,
Whatever seasons roll,
Still darkness drags along each dreary lingering
hour.

Angels of mercy! man to man a slave,
　　Chain'd, fetter'd to a senseless stone!
　　Perennial punishment! his life a groan!
His days a lengthen'd night, his antidote the
　　grave!

Is there no period in the womb of fate
　　(Time lash thy coursers, haste the happy year!)
When War and Tyranny shall terminate
　　The eclat of their mad career?
When pride from his high monument shall fall,
And *all* shall recognize the dynasty of *all!*

Yes, Independence, 'tis thy sacred fire
　　Lures resignation to the human breast:
　　　　And sweet Content with her exhaustless
　　　　store,
And dove-like Patience that can never tire,
　　Into thy lap their endless blessings pour,
　　A rich an everlasting feast.

And he who shares thy spirit may foretel,
Tho' doubly lock'd in adamantine cell,
   Some glorious era yet unborn,
   But whose illustrious morn
Shall soon arise, and with unrival'd light
Dispel the mental gloom of Superstition's night!
Old Prejudice shall from his antique throne
Descend, and all his former follies own;
Oh, who can tell the blessings of that time!
No title then shall sanctify a crime;
No ponderous load of laws perplex the truth,
No murderous wars destroy our rising youth,
No leeches of corruption bleed the state,
No languid luxuries enerve the great,
No wretch depend on chance for kind relief,
No feudal vassal, no orgillous chief!
On every continent, on every isle,
Shall independant Man look up and smile!

INVOCATION TO PEACE.

QUEEN of the Lyre, celestial Peace!
Where dost thou hide thy smiling face?
   Why dost thou yet avert thy sun-like eye,
      From Albion's shore?
      Wilt thou no more
    Re-visit her salubrious sky?
Hast thou no nerve in thy fair frame,
  Whose thrilling fibres shall convey
    Unto thy feeling heart,
  Want's trembling eager plea?
    Whose soft vibration's shall impart
The Patriot's fervent prayer,
The Orphan's cry, the Widow's tear?
Rob'd in the dreadful gloom of night,
   Despair stalks thro' our land!
Monster too hideous for human sight!

And in his frightful train,
That sweeps along the groaning plain,
Ah! see, in gorgon terrors clad,
Gigantic Hunger rave along,
With mien distorted, actions mad;
With desperate sinewy arm, and ever clamorous
tongue!
And see, close at his heels advance,
With hands imbru'd in blood, and huge uplifted
lance,
A savage monster with unmeaning face:
Nor in his actions may you trace
The foul complottings of his heart,
He flings his fatal dart,
With rancour indiscriminate,
Against the objects of his love, the victims of his
hate:
'Tis Anarchy! of Babel birth,
Pregnant with every plague thy votaries fear;
O! drive him headlong from the earth,
And War, his furious mad compeer!

O come, sweet Peace, and be our guest,
　　And give our land a lasting rest :
Hast thou so soon forgot the welcome cheer
　　　　We gave thee here,
When War and death Columbia's sons defy'd?
　　　　Let not the pride
　　　　Of our internal foes,
　　　　Thy tranquil reign oppose ;
ʹ Let not Intrigue with double tongue,
　　Nor base Corruption's golden shower,
With selfish views adroit, prolong
　　The triumphs of the hostile hour.
Return, sweet Peace, and cheer each sinking heart,
And from our native Isle, O never more depart!

MISCELLANIES.

ON

THE PLEASURES OF RETIREMENT.

OH Disappointment, vex my soul no more,
  The goal of Fortune is Retirement's cot;
There would I hide me from thy scornful power,
  " The world forgetting, by the world forgot."

In Nature's virgin prospects let me stray,
  Unbroke the glebe, untrod the pastures green;
For only anxious strife, and wild dismay,
  Attend this busy inharmonious scene:

Here flattering Hope decoys the weary mind,
  Anticipation revels in delight,
But dark Despair for ever hangs behind,
  Wrapt in the gloom of Disappointment's night.

For ever green and fair to thee, fond youth,
   The distant hills of Happiness arise;
Fame's lofty temple, and the fane of Truth,
   With tears of joy o'erswell thy longing eyes:

No canker-worm of Prejudice or Pride,
   No calls of interest or suspicious fear,
No superstitious dreams, have yet destroy'd
   The generous impulse of an heart sincere.

Imagination's vigour scorns controul,
   While mimic Fancy, wild delusive maid,
With visionary bliss o'erwhelms the soul,
   And mocks Reflection's wisely offer'd aid.

Hope's Sun effulgent shines; thy radiant morn
   With health, and innocence, and joy, is crown'd;
These, that the body and the mind adorn,
   With youth and virtue, flourish and abound.

But ah! they're gone, with youth is virtue fled,
  The charm's dissolv'd, the goodly prospect dies,
By Manhood is mis-shap'd Misfortune led ;
  With rising years unnumbered cares arise.

What heart by Nature's simple dictates sway'd,
  What eyes to soft Compassion's influence
    known,
But weeps for misery, by misfortune made,
  But feels that misery as it feels its own ?

And O how rare to see Compassion grow,
  Where Plenty spreads her costly viands round?
How seldom does the tear of pity flow,
  Where Power, and Wealth, and Luxury are
    found ?

But not the tender heart or weeping eye,
  Nor all the soothing arts Compassion knows,
Can slay the wants of wretched Poverty,
  Or give to Hunger's form a calm repose.

Who then with Nature's gifts profusely stor'd,
  Can live to see her violated shame?
To see her rubbish and her dross ador'd,
  By venal parasites of Wealth and Fame?

Come then with me and seek the silent grove,
  The rural lawn and hermitage obscure,
There with Content for ever may'st thou rove,
  From worldly noise and worldly strife secure.

The echoing dale, the gently rising hill,
  With rustic innocence more joys afford,
Than to the feeble Beau, the actor's skill,
  Than to the Miser's eye, the golden hoard.

Can splendid theatres or stores of wealth,
  Such various charms as blooming Nature boast?
Can wit or sordid treasures purchase health,
  Or stands Content at haughty Honour's post?

Behold the peaceful shades and rural bowers,
  Where Nature's feather'd songsters warble wild,
Where gentle breezes fan the candent hours,
  The mornings healthy, and the evenings mild.

Here Love and Friendship, such as *Shenstone* sung,
  May wing the hours in calm repose away,
Nor wilt thou think the passing moments long,
  When cold December gives his darkest day.

Here may'st thou shun infernal War's delight,
  The shrieks of Murder and the Trumpet's blast!
Here bury in Oblivion's endless night,
  The numerous ills of life already past.

Here may'st thou feed on wisdom's sacred lore,
  And woo fair Science to thy calm retreat,
And when the howling winds tempestuous roar,
  Defy the storms of Life's uncertain fate.

The sneer of tinsel Pride, the great man's scorn,
  Sensations of contempt no more impart;
Affected consequence by Folly worn,
  No more offends the eye or grieves the heart.

Here may aspiring Contemplation feed
  On Nature's banquets, or sublimely soar
Where bold Imagination dares to lead,
  Beyond the boundaries of this mundane shore!

And humble Piety of heavenly birth,
  Shall learn thee Resignation's calm delight,
Shall raise thy thoughts above the cares of earth,
  And point to everlasting realms of light!

Adieu, then, all ye tantalizing toys
  The world calls pleasures, I abandon you,
I only seek for intellectual joys!
  Once more vain world—a long—a last adieu!

ELEGIAC VERSES

On the Death of a young Man, who died of a consumption in his twentieth year, and whose labour supported his infirm and widow'd Mother, and a Sister blind from her birth.

SAY, shall the Youth to Poverty a prey,
   In Memory's cabinet no corner find?
Shall the fair virtues of an early day,
   Leave no chaste lesson to the world behind?

Forbid it friendship, and esteem sincere,
   Forbid it honour,—yes, and thou cold grave,
Silent spectator of the falling tear,
   The grateful elegy of truth dost crave.

What tho' the annals of the brave and great,
   Tell not Futurity his deeds of worth,
What tho' Biography shall ne'er relate,
   With scrup'lous pen, the moment of his birth:

And what if partial Science did deny
    Those gifts fair Wisdom gives her to bestow,
Or Independence, with unmoisten'd eye,
    Beheld him agonize with human woe!

Yet shall his virtues be the more rever'd,
    Tho' wrapt in Poverty's forbidding guise,
By those who slight them evermore be fear'd,
    But lov'd and cherish'd by the truly wise.

If Perseverance merits true esteem;
    If filial Piety commands respect;
If manly Fortitude with eye serene,
    And Patience to endure unjust neglect:

If these deserve one sympathizing tear,
    When doom'd to sink obscurely in the dust,
O children of Compassion, drop it here!
    When Virtue calls, the tribute is but just.

. And you, whom custom proudly calls the great,
    And you as vain the appellation wear,
No more affect disdain for low estate,
    Or virtue wedded to distress and care.

For he whose memory the Muse would sing,
    Well knew the soft emotions of the breast,
His heart would vibrate to the softest string,
    His tongue would soothe the weary soul to rest.

True to those bonds which Nature ever gives,
    But frequent Vice erases from the mind,
On the small pittance of his labour lives
    An helpless parent, and a sister blind.

Forth to his toil, soon as the wakeful morn
    With unheard steps came dancing o'er the dew,
He comes, complaisant cheerfulness is worn
    Upon his cheeks, altho' of sickly hue.

At length Disease, with his infectious train
    Consumptive, wears his lingering life away;
O God of Mercy! rack'd with torturing pain,
    On earth he now implores a longer stay.

To chase with anxious zeal the haggard forms
    Of Want and Famine from a parent's eyes!
To avert with guardian arm the angry storms
    That in the lands of Penury arise!

It cannot be,—Death strikes his fatal dart:
    O Muse, thou saw'st the victim on his bier;
Thou saw'st the anguish of her aching heart,
    Who could not see—but felt the falling tear.

But ah! no softly sympathizing strain
    Of earthly harmony can joy impart;
No muse of sorrow speak a parent's pain,
    Or soothe the pangs that rend a sister's heart.

SONNET TO THE AVON.

WHETHER by Sol's bright beam, or Cyn-
    thia's ray,
  Or does the Lark or Philomela sing,
Sweet stream, if on thy verdant banks I stray,
  Still joys ideal rise on Fancy's wing.

How grateful to the contemplative mind,
  To muse beside thy sinuous tranquil tide,
Where Love forlorn and Poesy may find
  Such joys as Innocence can there provide.

In thy transparent current, Virtue fair,
  Beholds Content with heavenly smiling mien,
But Vice, unseemly Vice, has only seen
  The horrid forms of Envy and Despair.
For he whose heart from guilt is wholly free,
Shall glide along Life's vale as calm as thee.

SONNET TO A FALLEN OAK.

PRIDE of the forest, beauty of the dale !
   Whose wide extended arms with foliage gay,
Lent a new odour to the morning gale,
   And crown'd with fresher wreath the rosy May:

Full oft beneath thy friendly shade reclin'd,
   Thy leaves still hung with Morn's ambrosial dew,
I carv'd each name to Love or Friendship true,
   Now hid with Moss, or with fond Ivy twin'd.

Alas! now prostrate—firm unbending tree,
   What ruthless hand has torn thy bark away?
'Twas Av'rice dealt the blow—by *Fate's* decree,
   That watch'd thy growth, and mark'd thee for
      his prey.
To *Fate's* resistless stroke *alone* resign'd,
Fit emblem of the firm and independent mind.

ELEGIAC SONNET.

THE star of Eve with silver lustre shone,
When lo! beside a crystal fount was seen
A youth,—(sad victim of despair I ween)
With folded arms,—all listless and alone,
And thus was heard to pour his plaintive moan,
As nearer he approach'd the margin green :
" And Oh! fair spring," he said, " thy verdant
        " scene,
" Thy gushing waters—and thy mossy stone,
" Where whilom wont my pensive heart to cheer,
" But now to griefs incurable a prey ;
" No more I come around thy banks to stray,
" I come to end at once my sorrows here ;
" Then let me hide beneath thy friendly wave,
" Oh! let me rest, though in a wat'ry grave!"

CYLANDER AND LAURA.

A TALE.

WHERE thou of Owen's Vale, where is thy
    reed,
  That pour'd such tender wailings o'er the plain?
Oh! that the tyrant marble would recede,
    And give thy Muse or thee to earth again.

Oft in thy rural glades, and blooming bowers,
    Cylander taught his youthful feet to stray,
But ah! how swift, how fleeting were the hours,
    That brought delights so pure, and scenes so gay.

Cylander's was that happy middle state,
    Nor ere to want, nor ere to wealth allied;
The great he envied not, his soul was great,
    And virile Independence was his pride.

If Virtue's tranquil mien his eye beheld,
   Tho' in the gyves of penury confin'd,
No baits of pride or negligence withheld,
   From Friendship honest, and attention kind.

Too soon, alas! his unsuspecting breast
   Was taught to bear his own vindictive woes,
Too soon health-wasting Sorrow was his guest,
   Too soon his days of hope and pleasure close.

Laura, the boast of many a lyric song,
   The blooming Laura won his tender heart,
Her graceful charms employ'd his willing tongue
   In strains which admiration would impart.

In the sincere effusions of his muse,
   Behold what energies inspir'd his mind;
Read, but let virtuous Candour well excuse
   Those faults superior excellence may find.

CYLANDER TO LAURA.

Descend, celestial Muse, inspire my song,
  And while my raptur'd breast invokes thy aid,
Rise far superior to the vulgar throng,
  Superior as the theme, superior as the maid!

    What time the conscious heart receives,
    The deep impression beauty gives;
    What time the willing eyes impart
    These inward motions of the heart;
    'Tis his to tune the trembling lyre,
    That dares approach the optic fire,
And dares to joys and bliss unknown aspire!

Not so the Muse her love—her fear
Forbids the bold, the mad career,
Unequall'd to the daring flight
She must sink to endless night;
Her humble strains, and humbler birth
Can never hope to gain such worth,
For he who aims to *merit* heaven shall sink be-
neath the earth.

The Mendicant forlorn and poor
Well knows thy hospitable door,
And when his shivering limbs appear,
The smother'd sigh, the hasty tear,
Proclaim thy gentle heart to bleed
For him whose only crime is need;
This shall be known on earth, and heaven reward
the deed.

The crimson blush, the downcast eye,
The sacred veil of Modesty;

The placid smile, the courteous mien,
Thy humble converse and demean,
Will more declare thý worth divine,
Than all this feeble praise of mine,
These shall thy happiness secure,
When lingering Time shall be no more,
And even thy pure form shall be more pure!

When sacred duties urge their way,
Serene and constant as the day
Appears the nymph whom duty calls
Within the circuit of her walls,
Learns to revere religious lore,
That when life's fleeting joys are o'er
She may with Angels like herself adore!

The Muse would fain the theme prolong,
And to the Heavens exalt her song,
But Fate has pass'd the stern decree,
Nor left one gleam of hope for me;

Yet while one spark of life remains,
 Or beats my pulse, or flow my veins,
I still must love and still repeat my strains.

 And should Compassion wish to know
 The hapless youth, the child of woe;
 'Tis him whose melancholy bears
 No kind proportion to his years,
 Whose whole deportment marks Despair,
 With solemn gate, and pensive air,
 And seeks retirement, tho' the child of Care.

She read, she pitied, and she lov'd the swain,
 But what could Pity, what could Love avail?
When iron-hearted Wealth with high disdain,
 Scoff'd his low birth and scorn'd his simple tale?

Yet Love and Pity urg'd a kind return,
 And triumph'd o'er the blandishments of art;
She wrote, and even blind Love may well discern
 A pure ingenuous mind a feeling heart.

" I'm not a stranger to your worth," she said,
    " Your great, your many virtues I revere,
" The accident of birth can ne'er degrade,
    " Can ne'er exalt, we fragile mortals here;

" The glare of wealth no merit can impart:
    " But Oh, Cylander! think me not unkind,
" I would not grieve an aged parent's heart,
    " Tho' life itself were in the cause resign'd.

" And had Cylander, had wise Heaven ordain'd
    " In the same path of life our feet should move,
" I'd hail thy virtues, and with joys unfeign'd,
    " Fly to thy arms on the chaste wings of love.

" Mine is the loss, for wealth can ne'er bestow
    " Such constant love, such real worth as thine,
" Tho' resignation in my breast may glow,
    ," Indifference never—never can be mine!

" An aged parent's life on me depends,
   " I am her only hope, her last frail prop,
" The first dark hour that disobedience sends,
   " Must see her faltering frame in anguish drop.

" Adieu, Cylander—rouse thy generous soul
   " Above the influence of this hapless flame,
" Let Reason, Passion's boisterous storm controul,
   " Nor give parental love too harsh a name."

With eager eye Cylander read his fate,
   Love swell'd his breast, and roll'd the streaming
      tear,
" Oh! 'tis too much, I could have borne her hate,
   " But ah! this cruel love I cannot bear;

" What can a parent's fondest wish require,
   " More than Content and Competence can give?
" Abundance gluts the keenness of desire,
   " Fame, Grandeur, Power, and Affluence can
      but live.

" What name too harsh for folly frail and blind,
  " My Laura, Age and Ignorance may assume
" Dominion o'er the virtuous free-born mind,
  " But Reason points undaunted to their tomb.

" Maternal love I ever must revere,
  " Obedience dutiful I must esteem,
" Victim of virtues amiably austere,
  " Complainings may too like injustice seem.

" In the same path of life we surely tread,
  " In Virtue's path, for only two are given,
" The one to sharp remorse and woe will lead,
  " The other leads to happiness and heaven.

" But ah! 'tis wealth must purchase thee, my fair;
  " Oh then ten thousand mines of gold I crave,
" An Emperor's diadem! Golconda's glare!
  " And all that Waste can spend or Avarice save?

" What, then, is Beauty venal! O my heart
    " Reject the thought, and hear the calls of love;
" To distant climes she bids thee now depart,
    " In quest of Happiness and Wealth to rove.

" Of Happiness? Ah no! 'tis here alone,
    " 'Tis only Laura can that bliss bestow;
" But Wealth! can Wealth for Happiness atone?
    " It must:—for Wealth—for Laura, then I go."

And o'er the Ocean vast he took his way,
    And many a boist'rous storm of life he bore,
Not only swelling o'er the fickle sea,
    But o'er his troubled mind on *India's* shore.

'Neath scorching suns, mid burning atmospheres,
    Remembering still his Laura, 'there he strove
With unremitting zeal for seven long years,
    To obtain the price of happiness and love.

And long she bore his image on her mind,
   For well she knew the purpose of his breast;
Till Perfidy and Avarice combin'd
   Their hellish frauds, as Truth and Virtue drest,

And forg'd his death, and urg'd the weeping maid
   To obey her aged mother's fond desire;
" That such ignoble tears must low degrade
   " The virtuous memory of her honour'd sire."

At length, to ease a parent's anxious fear,
   And calm the welkin of her evening hours,
(Tho' tempest threaten her own hemisphere,
   And every moment with misfortune lowers.)

She yields her listless hand—no more she gave,
   For love, alas! she had not to bestow;
And oft her hesitating mind misgave
   Some near approach of wretchedness and woe.

That day, that fatal day Cylander came,
   " Fraught with abundance now of sordid ore;
" No more," says he, " shall Pride dispute my claim,
   " Or glittering Grandeur spurn me from his door:

" 'Tis well, ye merry bells, your cheerful peal
   " Suit well my beating heart, suit well the day
" I meet again my Laura, and reveal
   " My undiminish'd love, and her's repay."

He sought with hasty steps the well-known door,
   He saw his Laura wreath'd with garland's gay;
" Cylander!"—" Laura! Why this garland wore?
   " Ah me!—her lips are pale—she dies away!"

Oh leave the scene, Imagination fails,
   Humanity recoils to Virtue's seat,
Grandeur is deaf, and therefore what avails
   To paint the sorrows of this world's estate?

Cylander lives, but ah, he lives in vain,
    Reason subdu'd has fled her royal throne,
And hot distemper'd blood boils thro' each vein,
    Nor joy nor sorrow to his heart is known!

In furious tone for Laura now he raves,
    And now with suppliant voice on Fortune calls,
Now blames the tardy winds and envious waves,
    And now with desperate fury beats the walls!

Alike to him the frigid northern blast
    And southern gale, the world's esteem and hate,
For all his hours of happiness are past,
    And Pity can but weep his hapless fate.

MOON-LIGHT.

A POEM.

MARK how the day-light glides away,
Following Sol's departed ray;
The shades of Night come on a pace,
And Cynthia shews her lovely face!
Welcome, thou lenient Queen of night,
I love thy reign, I love thy light,
In some romantic dell to stray,
And there forget the busy day;
All earthly sorrow to forego,
A world of care, a world of woe,
And muse beside some purling stream,
Whose face reflects thy mildest beam;
The wonders of the welkin scan,
And ponder o'er the state of man;
Raise my faint thought to deity,
And think of Heaven and look at thee!

Or give me some old ruin'd tower
To pass my contemplative hour,
Midst broken turrets, mouldering walls,
Porches antique, and echoing halls;
Where other feet shall never stray,
Nor other sounds but thy sweet lay,
Nocturnal warbler Philomel,
Thy grateful antiphons shall swell
With pious rapture to the skies,
And teach my grov'ling thoughts to rise.

Here seated on some moss-clad stone,
The weary Pilgrim sits alone,
Beneath that hanging arch's shade
His fervent orisons were paid;
And there upon that scatter'd hay
He slept the darkness all away,
Rose with the morning's early gale,
And soon devour'd his scanty meal;
Then o'er his back he flings his store,
Nor seeks his habitation more.

Here then I'll sit—advance each spright,
Each lonely spectre of the night.

With folded arms and downcast eye,
See Melancholy gliding by !
How slow her step—how pale her mien !
'Tis said she likes not to be seen ;
Yet many mortals, sick with woe,
Abandon Hope with her to go ;
She leads them o'er the blasted heath
And wilds forlorn—and talks of death;
And when the tempest rolls above
She leads them to the thickest grove ;
Or where these wrecks of time are found
She often treads the hallow'd ground ;
Or 'neath her plant, the yew-tree's shade,
Among the mansions of the dead ;
There with her votaries will she stay,
Till gloomy night is chas'd away !
But stay, sad child of cankering care,
Of she and all her arts beware ;

Break, break her charm, her potent spell,
And thou shalt see a fiend of hell!
With daggers arm'd, stalk by her side;
His hated name is Suicide!
O hapless fate, yet oft 'tis true,
Her votaries are his victims too!

See! see! a second form appears,
A frantic countenance he wears;
He starts! looks! hesitates—and then
With hurry'd pace goes on again;
His mirror magnifies all care
An hundred fold! His name Despair!
More fouler fiend—more horrid spright
Ne'er haunts the dreary gloom of night.
In vain for him the Nightingale
Carols her sweet and plaintive tale;
His sullen ear will only pay
Attention to the screech-owl's lay:
His eye, fair Cynthia, hates thy light,
And only loves the stormy night,

And when the vivid lightnings glare,
And Heaven and Earth appear at war!
With impious scorn defying life,
He seeks the elemental strife;
And when the wrathful surges roar,
And proudly dash the rocky shore,
Furious he climbs its craggy side,
And there he mocks the foaming tide!
But O! frail Man, beware his power,
Or else in some unguarded hour,
When watchful Reason's lull'd to sleep,
He'll dash thee headlong down the steep,
To perish in the briny deep!

Creation's mute! How still the trees!
Hush'd is the gently murmuring breeze,
The bird of night has ceas'd her song;
The village cur that bark'd so long,
With clamorous throat and surly grin,
Has weary'd Echo with his din.

No sounds along the ether float,
Finish'd the screech-owl's guttural note;
Ravens and Bats have ceas'd their flight,
And left the world to me and Night.
Come then dread Silence, leave thy cell,
Look me those thoughts thou canst not tell:
She comes! what dignity! what grace!
How grave, how reverend her face!
Unfit for Heaven, too good for Earth,
Yon gloomy cavern gave her birth;
Her parents, natives of that wood,
Reflection and grave Solitude,
(Let none their birth obscure deride)
With unheard steps tread by her side,
O pious trio! who can say,
How wise, how truly blest are they,
Who pall'd with worldly strife and noise,
Retire and taste your mental joys.
Let fawning parasites then prate
About the splendors of the great;

Let simp'ring courtiers mimic folly,
Slaves or to Mirth or Melancholy;
One frown may all their prospects blast,
So soon their transient joys are past;
Just like a comet is their story,
Dazzling the glare but short the glory.
And so may vain Ambition shine,
And boast his actions quite divine!
Swell to a giant in opinion,
As he relates his vast dominion;
And puff'd and bloated with conceit,
Mountains of fame accumulate!
O twins of folly, and of guilt,
What baseless fabric have you built?
Monsters of Nature! but intrude
Into these haunts of Solitude,
And all your charms shall shrink away
As lightnings blast the bloom of May.
Silence affords no joys for you,
And stern Reflection hates you too,

For he will probe the human heart,
Nor heeds the groan, nor feels the smart;
Remorse and Shame extracting thence,
He heals the wounded moral sense.
And 'tis sedate Reflection's power
To feed the contemplative hour,
With viands suited to the taste
Of Man alone,—deny'd the beast.
Teach me thy solemn serious lore,
I'll con thy sage instructions o'er;
With never-tiring zeal I'll tread
Where thy mysterious paths shall lead;
And taught by thee, I'll learn to scan
The powers and properties of Man,
His reason's intellectual soul,
His hopes, his prospects, and his goal;
How short, how frail his present state,
And yet how wonderful how great!
Sure these will argue Man has life
Beyond this vale of toil and strife;

Sure these proclaim some happier sphere,

Congenial with his wishes here.

Shall he whose thoughts surmount the sky,

In the cold grave for ever lie?

Forbid it Hope and Reason too,

And Hope and Reason ever do.

But 'tis not Hope alone is given,

To point us to some future Heaven.

Recoil, ye infidels, beware!

Ten thousand potent proofs appear,

In history, sacred and profane;

Be not so confident—so vain.

Knowledge may spread her pinions wide,

And Reason swell with every tide;

Science and Liberty may smile

On every continent and isle;

But these can ne'er eclipse that truth

That cheers the sage and awes the youth.

Are frightful errors on the earth?

With Truth and Reason drive them forth;

But ne'er let doubts and vague surmise,
Thy great capacious mind suffice.
Come, infidel, to this lone place,
(If thou canst come with serious face)
For solemn is this ruin'd scene,
Because it tells us what *has* been.
Dost thou behold this orb of night,
Whose beams so sweetly court thy sight?
Then turn thy eyes to that dark shade
Where many a valiant knight is laid,
Whose martial prowess, and whose might
Conspicuous shone in barbarous fight,
Who in this self-same spot has stood
And view'd, as we do now the wood;
And cannot he who built this sky,
And form'd those stars that daze the eye,
Who plac'd that planet there at first,
Raise a frail mortal from the dust?
His power who doubts, his will is known,
By Jesus Christ, his only son.

Or think'st thou Chance has form'd these spheres,
And roll'd them round six thousand years?
Chance then is order, and thy faith.
Belies what grateful Nature saith.
Away! thy creed is only guess,
Lost in Conjecture's wilderness.

Now Midnight's dark and gloomy sway,
Chills the traveller with dismay;
Clouds heap'd on clouds advance apace,
And veil the bloom of Cynthia's face;
The bellowing winds aloud complain,
As drives the dreadful hurricane,
The forked lightnings dart around,
And midnight thunders shake the ground.
O Darkness! hide me in thy cell,
Tho' mock'd by Fear, with thee I'll dwell,
'Till this rude storm has pass'd away,
And Cynthia's night shall rival day;
Hail sepulchre of optic bliss!
Thy blear dank cavern welcome is

When images of dire despair
Ride triumphant thro' the air;
Ah! many a sigh and many a groan
Arise from dungeons quite thy own;
Ev'n in the midst of life an light,
Tyrants have form'd and endless night,
Where arbiters of human fate
Like fiends they torture those they hate.
Search sons of Liberty awhile
The annals of your boasted Isle,
See if no patriot blood has flow'd
Unpitied for the public good!
Has Genius never been confin'd
To cramp the ardour of the mind?
RALEIGH, too late we now lament
Thy undeserved punishment;
Bold SYDNEY's fire, and HAMPDEN's zeal,
Shall make us more than pity feel;
Britannia's self shall execrate
Her SYDNEY's and her HAMPDEN's fate.

Wrapt in false visions of the brain,
Hear Superstition's voice complain!
With apprehensive fear half dead,
His own dark thoughts create his dread;
And now, when full-orb'd Cynthia reigns,
He mopes along the silent plains;
He loves monasteries obscure,
Forgot by fickle fame and power;
And there he heaves the forced sigh,
And there he rolls his heavy eye,
That ceases not to overflow
From inward pangs of fancy'd woe;
With grief-worn face, (a stale pretence)
The counterfeit of penitence;
Abased, sordid, passive, fool,
Buffoon of Reason's sov'reign school;
The bitter enemy of mirth,
Thou foe of Heaven, pest of earth,
When art was rude and science young,
Man heard the clamours of thy tongue;

K

He heard ! and Reason's mental light
Quickly vanish'd from his sight.
O ! blind to Nature's cheerful smile !
For Superstition to beguile;
A monster, whose ignoble mind
No delights for man could find !
'Twas him whose base tumultuous breath,
When Sinai's summit menac'd death,
Proclaim'd idolatry aloud,
Beneath the Almighty's thund'ring cloud.
And he, when OMAR'S * raving zeal
Disdain'd fair Learning's chaste appeal,
Remorseless gave to raging flames
Her bright, her most illustrious names;
Infernal Demon ! not to save
Heaven-born Science from the grave !
And many a CARTHAGINIAN slain,
Pollutes the annals of thy reign.

* The Mahometan Caliph, who commanded the
Philadelphian Library to be burnt.

Relentless fiend! to boast the deed
When infants cry! when children bleed!
At MECCA's oriental shrine
I hear thy bigot votaries pine;
Pedestrian saints in rags appear,
(Their zeal revolving with the year)
For there thy darling prophet told,
Of heavenly wonders manifold;
There rais'd his barbarous tyrant throne,
Worthy of Mahomet alone;
And thence his oral mandates hurl'd
With vengeance o'er the eastern world!
And didst not thou assistance yield,
And arm his warriors for the field,
When Terror, nurs'd in fire and blood,
Beside his haughty banners stood?
Didst not thou in his van appear?
Rapine and Murder in his rear?
While mad Ambition stalk'd before,
With garments dy'd in human gore!

K 2

And every plague that hurts mankind,
With Devastation, lurk'd behind!
Hell's native fury victory gains,
Wild horror shrieks along the plains;
Keen anguish every heart doth seize,
Death triumphs! temples, cities blaze!
Nor ASIA's swarthy sons alone
Have bow'd before thy bubble throne,
Europa's fairest vales have seen
Thy giant form and hideous mien:
Europe, that boasts of creeds divine,
Where sacred truths immortal shine,
Where Science spreads her mental feast
For every willing friend to taste;
Where all the sister arts resort,
And Reason holds his sober court;
Inexorable fiend! Behold!
Her sanguine history unfold,
Murders! assassinations dire!
Racks, tortures, faggots, gibbets, fire!

See saints like DUNSTAN domineer,
BONNERS and RAVAILLACS appear;
Monks, jesuits, and canting friars,
Popes, cardinals, and sainted liars!
These thy dependants, nurs'd in guile,
In secret vice, and actions vile,
Impugn each moral law that's given
By sage philosophers or heaven.
In public streets and pulpits mild,
Pure, innocent, and undefil'd,
In convents bacchanalian's rude,
Proud, insolent, rapacious, lew'd;
Agents of homicide, unknown
To heed the wretched's dying groan.
O ye who plung'd the murdering steel,
O ye who turn'd the torturing wheel,
Prepar'd the fierce tormenting fire,
Or sear'd the flesh with burning wire;
Or ye of Albion's favour'd isle
Who rear'd the Christian's funeral pile,

Why, wretches, could you not descry
Posterity's impartial eye;
And read, in Reason's copious page,
The curse of every future age?
Away, fell Sorcerer, from this scene!
And never let thy form be seen
To haunt the temple's sacred bounds,
Muttering strange portentous sounds;
Or with utopian shadows glide
In rustic hamlets lonely, wild,
In armor'd halls, and houses drear,
To picture gorgon shapes for fear;
Fly, for base Ignorance, thy sire,
Shall soon with mortal wounds expire!
Fly to Oblivion's torpid shore,
And vex the race of man no more.

But come, dear Friendship, thou canst find
A balm for every wounded·mind;
Come, tread these lonely paths with me,
For Disappointment knows not thee;

Come then, Philander, come and tell
Where gay Contentment loves to dwell,
And (if thou know'st her bless'd retreat)
Lead, O lead me to her seat;
Memory calls those happy days,
When Friendship never fail'd to please,
Each summer's-eve, when tasks were done,
The rural walk, by setting sun,
Or glimmering moonlight, well repaid
Our daily toil, beneath the shade
Of * * *'s grove; and be it mine
For thee, Philander, less to shine,
Less to my sublunary end,
Less as the poet than the friend.

But see the day begins to dawn,
Now flitting o'er the upland lawn,
Streaming the horizon round,
Till Cynthia's borrowed light is drown'd
With orient rays of dazzling light;
Scouting the phantoms of the night,

The glorious sun climbs up the sky
And flings his beams in every eye;
The   ouring voice of Chanticleer,
Piercing every slumbering ear,
Summons rude labour from his cot,
And wakes mime Echo in his grot.
Adieu, ye tranquil silent shades,
Ye soothing rills and verdant glades,
Now duty calls to toil and strife,
Yet duty is the friend of life.
A few more views of night and day,
Of glimmering morn, and evening grey,
And then the scene shall roll away.
A few more storms of misery brave,
And then thy shelter is the grave;
And there the Muse must drop her wing,
Nor ever more to soar, nor ever more to sing.

HYMN FOR NEW YEAR's DAY.

As years revolve, as seasons roll,
Exert thy latent powers, my soul;
To God thy great creator raise
Anthems of never ending praise.

When blooming Spring revives the earth,
And casts her fragrant odours forth,
With sweetest melody of tongue,
With grateful heart revive thy song.

Or when resplendent Summer reigns,
And Plenty smiles upon the plains,
Let every gentle breeze that's given
Convey some note of praise to heaven.

When bounteous Autumn spreads abroad
The blessings of our gracious God,
In some sublime his praise rehearse,
Whose arm sustains the universe.

When stormy Winter, bleak and drear,
Coldly concludes the varied year,
Still warm with gratitude proclaim
The wonders of Jehovah's name.

And ever as the morning shines,
Or as the weary day declines,
And ever as thy wants return,
Still may thy grateful ardour burn.

Great God, exert thy powerful hand,
Protect, preserve, our native land;
Still let thy love and grace appear
The guardians of each circling year.

FINIS.

LIST

OF

SUBSCRIBERS.

*** Those Names to which the Place of Residence is not affixed, reside in London.

Mr. Allen

Mr. Armistead, 2 copies

Rev. W. Amphlett, Towcester, 7 copies

Mr. T. Amphlett, Southwark

M. T. Amphlett, Birmingham

Mr. J. Amphlett, do. 2 copies

Mr. Atkins, do.

Mr. Bamford, Westmancoat, Worcestershire

Mr. Baker, Birmingham

Mr. W. Baker, do.

Mr. J. Beard, do.

Mr. Birch, Birmingham

Mr. W. Bennet, do.

Mr. A. Biggs, do.

Mr. T. Broomhead, do. 2 copies

Mr. Bliss, do.

Mr. H. Bynner, do.

Mr. J. Bynner, do.

Mr. Booth, Coventry

Mr. Bidlake, Kemerton, Worcestershire

Miss Best Eckington, do.

Mr. T. Breakwell

Mr. Camden, Birmingham

Mr. Clayton, do.

Mrs. Clayton, do.

Mr. Cash, Birmingham
Mr. E. Corn, do.
Mr. S. Corn, do.
Mr. Cross, do.
Mr. Cox, Alcester
Mr. R. Campion, Heath-encoate, Northamp-tonshire
Mr. Caporn, Hanslope, do.
Mr. Courtier, Hammer-smith
Miss Courtier, do.
Mr. P. Courtier, 2 co-pies
Mrs. Clark, Towcester
Mr. H. Clark
Mr. J. Clark
Mr. Clark, Thames-street
Mr. Clark, Birmingham
Mr. Crane
C. Chastenay, Esq.

Mr. S. Dobbs, West-mancoat, Worcester-shire
Miss M. Dobbs, do.
Miss E. Dudfield, do.

Mr. T. Deykin, Bir-mingham
Mr. R. Dobie, do.
Rev. E. Dawson, Eve-sham
Mr. W. Deykin
Mr. W. Dawkes, Ham-mersmith
Mr. Davis, Pershore
Mr. H. Dix
Mr. Dickens, Tiffield, Northamptonshire
Miss Dawkes, Walworth

Mr. Edwards, Birming-ham
Mr. Ellams, do.
Mr. Elliot, Westminster
Mr. J. Elt

Mr. W. Flavell, Bir-mingham
Mr. T. Fletcher, do.
Mr. Frazer, do. 5 copies
Miss Fossey, Hammer-smith
Mr. W. Forsyth, Ken-sington

LIST OF SUBSCRIBERS.

Mr. Fountain, Calcutta

J. Goold, Esq. Mile End

Mr. S. Gibbes, Towcester

Mr. J. Gibbes, do.

— Grant, Esq. do.

Mr. J. Goodman, do.

Mr. John Goodman, Slapton, Northamptonshire

Mr. J. Goodman, Bradden, do.

Mr. Goodridge, Blisworth, do.

Mr. R. Ganderton, Pershore

Mr. A. Garnet, Hammersmith

Mr. T. Hughes, Evesham, 2 copies

Mr. B. Hughes, Alcester

Mr. S. Hughes, 2 copies

— Hurt, Esq. Burlingham, Worcestershire

Mr. Haden, Birmingham

Mr. T. Halliday, Birmingham

Mr. Hesketh, do.,

Mr. Horton, do.

Mrs. Horton, do.

Mr. Hilditch, do.

Miss Hubbard, do.

Mr. Hill, do.

Mr. Hill, Deptford

— Hudson, Esq. Pershore

Mr. Hackett, do.

Mr. Hampton, Longdon, Worcestershire

Mr. W. Horne, Worcester, 7 copies

Mr. Howell, Windsor

Rev. W. Humphryes, Hammersmith

Mr. J. Hardwitch, Bermondsey

H. H. Kensington

J. H.

Mr. Hill

Mr. S. Hooper

Mr. T. Hodgetts

Mr. J. Hands, Towcester

Mr. J. Illige, Birmingham

Miss F. Jones, Birmingham

Mr. J. Jew, do. 2 copies

Mr. W. Jeyns, 2 copies

Mr. D. Jones, Burlingham, Worcestershire

Mr. T. Jones, Hammersmith

Mr. R. Jones, do.

Mr. J. Kettleby, Birmingham

Mr. T. Kettle, do.

Mr. J. Killminster, 2 copies

Mr. J. Kenrick, do.

Mr. B. Knight, Evesham

J. Lee, Esq. 6 copies

Mr. J. Laugh

Mr. Lucas

Mr. Langton, Tewkesbury

Rev. M. Masters, Paulers Pury, Northamptonshire

Mr. J. May, do.

Mr. J. Mawle, Kirby Grounds, Northamptonshire

Mr. Matthews, Birmingham

Mr. J. Mosely, do.

Mr. John Mosely, do.

Miss Middleton, Towcester

Mrs. Munn, Hammersmith

Mr. Morin

Mr. Marnham

Mr. Morley

Mr. Montier

Mr. P. Nind, Birmingham

Mr. J. Nind, do.

Mr. H. Nickholls, do.

Mr. Newman

Mr. S. Parr, 2 copies

Miss C. Parry, Hammersmith

Miss M. Parry, do.

Mr. J. Prosser, Birmingham

Mr. Pearcy, do.

Mr. T. Phipson, Birmingham, 2 copies
Mr. Potts, do.
Mr. R. Peart, do.
Mr. Pearce, Evesham
Mr. W. Prescott
Mrs. Pope, Bristol

Mrs. Roper, Bengworth, Worcestershire
Mrs. Rose, Birmingham
Mr. Rickards, do.
Mr. J. Robins, Paulers Pury, Northamptonshire
Miss Randle, Deptford

Rev. J. Smith, Pershore
Rev. E. Smith, Blockley
Mr. Smith, Birmingham
Mr. T. Smith, do.
Mrs. Scott, Hammersmith
J. Scott, Esq. do.
Mr. J. Scott, do.
Miss Scott, do.

Mr. J. Scott, Paulers Pury, Northamptonshire
Mr. M. Stenson, Kensington
Mr. Salter, Hammersmith
Mr. Saltkill

Mr. John Tight, Looton, Northamptonshire
Mrs. Tight, Kirby Grounds, do.

Rev. R. Winter, 3 copies
Mr. R. Wallis, Birmingham, 2 copies
Mr. Watred, do.
Mr. J. Ward, do.
Mr. W. Wheildon, do.
Mr. J. Williams, do.
Robert Wainewright, Gray's-inn-square, Esq.
Arnold Wainewright, Esq.
Mr. Waldron

Mr. Wathen, Kensington

Mr. R. Willoughby, Greenwich

Mr. B. Willoughby, Canterbury

Mr. Stephen Warwick, Rode, Northamptonshire

Mr. J. Wilmot

Mr. R. White

Mr. C. West, Northamptonshire

Mr. Willcox, Towcester, 2 copies

Mr. Wildman

Mr. L. Webb

Miss Yates